BIG FEELINGS
FEELING AFRAID

by Mary Lindeen

Norwood House Press

DEAR CAREGIVER, The *Beginning to Read* Big Feelings books support children's social and emotional learning (SEL). SEL has been proven to promote not only the development of self-awareness, responsibility, and positive relationships but also academic achievement.

Current research reveals that the part of the brain that manages emotion is directly connected to the part of the brain that is used in cognitive tasks such as problem solving, logic, reasoning, and critical thinking—all of which are at the heart of learning.

SEL is also directly linked to what are referred to as 21st Century Skills: collaboration, communication, creativity, and critical thinking. The books included in this SEL series offer an early start to help children build the competencies they need for success in school and life.

In each of these books, young children will learn how to recognize, name, and manage their own feelings while learning that everyone shares the same emotions. This helps them develop social competencies that will benefit them in their relationships with others, which in turn contributes to their success in school. As they read, children will also practice early reading skills by reading sight words and content vocabulary.

The reinforcements in the back of each book will help you determine how well your child understands the concepts in the book, provide different ideas for your child to practice fluency, and suggest books and websites for additional reading.

The most important part of the reading experience with these books—and all others—is for your child to have fun and enjoy reading and learning!

Sincerely,

Mary Lindeen

Mary Lindeen, Author

Norwood House Press
For more information about Norwood House Press please visit our website at www.norwoodhousepress.com or call 866-565-2900.
© 2022 Norwood House Press. Beginning-to-Read™ is a trademark of Norwood House Press.
All rights reserved. No part of this book may be reproduced or utilized in any form or by any means without written permission from the publisher.

Editor: Judy Kentor Schmauss   *Designer*: Sara Radka

Photo Credits: Getty Images: Bryan Allen, 9, Carol Yepes, 21, Cavan Images, 18, Elva Etienne, 5, Elva Etienne, 17, evgenyatamanenko, 19, EyeEm/chwn chay pi na ka se, 10, EyeEm/Esther Moreno Martinez, cover, 1, ImagesBazaar, 13, Jose A. Bernat Bacete, 3, ktaylorg, 22, Masafumi Nakanishi, 26, Milko, 25, Yellow Dog Productions, 14, Zia Soleil, 6

Library of Congress Cataloging-in-Publication Data has been filed and is available at catalog.loc.gov

Library ISBN: 978-1-68450-821-1   Paperback ISBN: 978-1-68404-667-6

Look at this spider!

Lots of people think spiders like this are scary.

Not everyone feels that way though.

Some people think spiders are cool!

Some people think this is a scary ride.

Other people love it!

People feel afraid of different things.

But everyone feels afraid of something.

Some people get very still and quiet when they feel afraid.

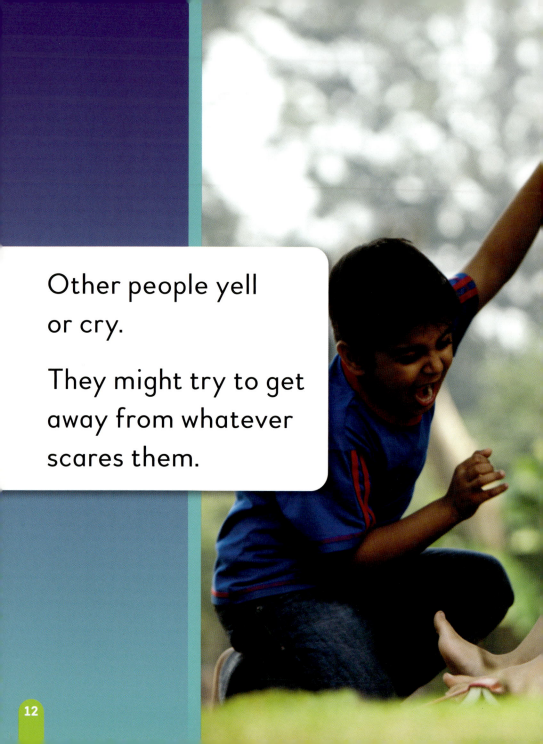

Other people yell or cry.

They might try to get away from whatever scares them.

Feeling afraid can make your heart beat faster.

It can make your eyes open wider and your muscles feel tight.

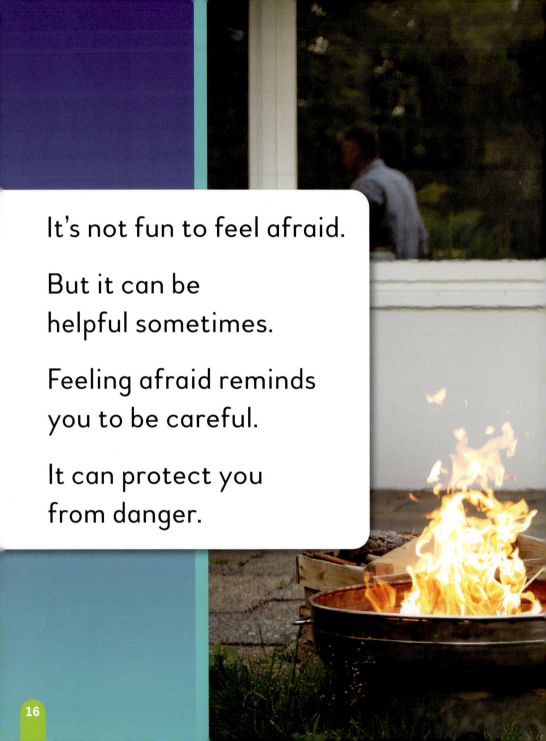

It's not fun to feel afraid.

But it can be helpful sometimes.

Feeling afraid reminds you to be careful.

It can protect you from danger.

But feeling afraid can also stop you from trying fun new things.

It helps to ask questions when you feel afraid.

Are your feelings keeping you safe?

Or are they making you too afraid to have fun?

Talking to someone you trust can help you feel less afraid.

Taking some deep breaths can be helpful, too.

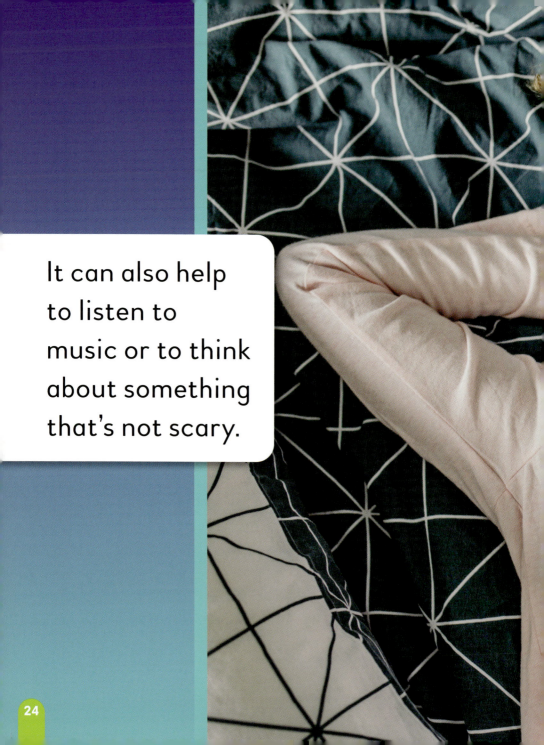

It can also help to listen to music or to think about something that's not scary.

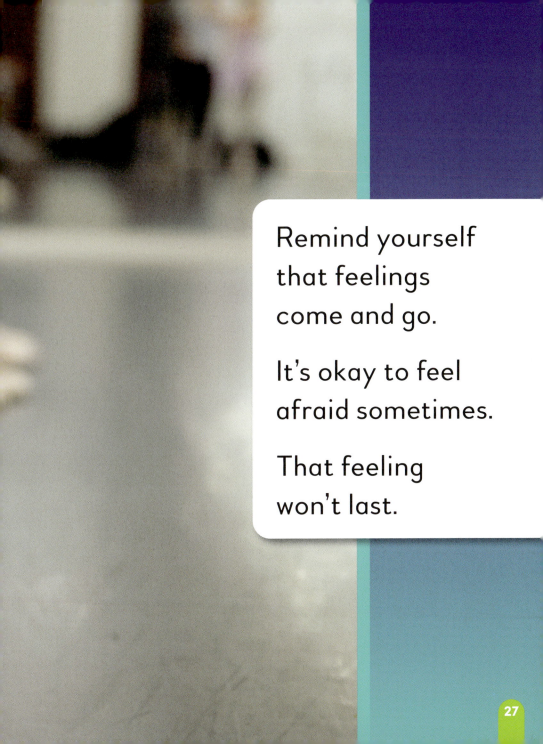

Remind yourself that feelings come and go.

It's okay to feel afraid sometimes.

That feeling won't last.

You'll feel better soon!

. . . READING REINFORCEMENT. . .

CONNECTING CONCEPTS

CLOSE READING OF NONFICTION TEXT

Close reading helps children comprehend text. It includes reading a text, discussing it with others, and answering questions about it. Use these questions to discuss this book with your child:

1. What does it mean to feel afraid?

2. Do you think grown-ups ever feel afraid? Why do you think so?

Once you have discussed the above questions, ask your child to either draw a picture of someone who is feeling afraid or choose one of the children pictured in the book. Then ask the following questions about the child in the drawing or the photo:

1. How can you tell this person might be feeling afraid?

2. What might be one reason this person is feeling afraid?

3. How would you feel in that situation?

4. Do you ever feel afraid? When?

5. When you feel afraid, what do you do? How could someone else help you when you're feeling afraid?

VOCABULARY AND LANGUAGE SKILLS

As you read the book with your child, make sure he or she understands the vocabulary used. Point to key words and talk about what they mean. Encourage children to sound out new words or to read the familiar words around an unfamiliar word for help reading new words.

FLUENCY

Help your child practice fluency by using one or more of the following activities:

1. Reread the book to your child at least two times while he or she uses a finger to track each word as it is read.

2. Read a line of the book, then reread it as your child reads along with you.

3. Ask your child to go back through the book and read the words he or she knows.

4. Have your child practice reading the book several times to improve accuracy, rate, and expression.

FURTHER READING FOR KIDS

Bullis, Amber. *Feeling Afraid*. Minneapolis, MN: Jump!, Inc., 2020.

Holmes, Kristy. *Feeling Afraid*. San Diego, CA: Kidhaven Publishing, 2018.

Morris, J.E. *Fish Are Not Afraid of Doctors*. New York, NY: Penguin Workshop, 2018.

FURTHER READING FOR TEACHERS/CAREGIVERS

Child Mind Institute: How to Help Children Manage Fears
https://childmind.org/article/help-children-manage-fears/

Johns Hopkins All Children's Hospital: Normal Childhood Fears
https://www.hopkinsallchildrens.org/Patients-Families/Health-Library/HealthDocNew/Anxiety-Fears-and-Phobias

KidsHealth: Normal Childhood Fears
https://kidshealth.org/en/parents/anxiety.html?WT.ac=ctg#catfeelings

Word List

Feeling Afraid uses the 99 words listed below. *High-frequency* words are those words that are used most often in the English language. They are sometimes referred to as sight words because children need to learn to recognize them automatically when they read. *Content* words are any words specific to a particular topic. Regular practice reading these words will enhance your child's ability to read with greater fluency and comprehension.

HIGH-FREQUENCY WORDS

a	different	making	things
about	from	might	think
also	get	not	this
and	go	of	to
are	have	or	too
ask	help(ful, s)	other	very
at	is	people	way
away	it	some	when
be	last	something	you
but	like	that	your
can	look	them	
come	make	they	

CONTENT WORDS

afraid	heart	quiet	that's
beat	it's	remind(s)	though
better	keeping	ride	tight
breaths	less	safe	trust
careful	listen	scares	try(ing)
cool	lots	scary	whatever
cry	love	someone	wider
danger	muscles	sometimes	won't
deep	music	soon	yell
everyone	new	spider(s)	you'll
eyes	okay	still	yourself
faster	open	stop	
feel(ing, ings, s)	protect	taking	
fun	questions	talking	

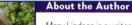

About the Author

Mary Lindeen is a writer, editor, parent, and former elementary school teacher. She has written more than 100 books for children and edited many more. She specializes in early literacy instruction and books for young readers, especially nonfiction.